This book belongs to:

JMCR

Contents

Cover illustration by Julie Anderson

A catalogue record for this book is available
from the British Library

Published by Ladybird Books Ltd
A subsidiary of the Penguin Group
A Pearson Company

© LADYBIRD BOOKS LTD MCMXCVII

LADYBIRD and the device of a Ladybird are trademarks of
Ladybird Books Ltd Loughborough Leicestershire UK

Seaside surprise

written by Marie Birkinshaw
illustrated by Julie Anderson

"Can **I** have the big spade now?" asked Anna.

"Here," said Matthew,
"but I'll need it again soon."

They were racing to make a giant sandcastle before the tide came in.

"Look, Dad! We've done it!" they shouted.

When the sea came up to them,
they all ran to the rocks.

They watched sadly as
the water flowed round
the castle walls.
Soon there was nothing left.

Suddenly they spotted
something in the water.

"Oh, no!" Anna shouted.
"We've left the big spade
behind."

"It's too late to get it now,"
Matthew said.

"We'll get it in the morning,"
said Dad.

Next day they looked everywhere. The tide was a really long way out and they found lots of interesting things in the rock pools.

Dad showed them some sea-snails, periwinkles, barnacles and dogwhelks. But they couldn't see the spade.

Anna, Matthew and Dad walked by some fishing boats.

"Look!" said Matthew. "That fisherman has a spade just like the one we lost in the sea."

"It's not mine!" said the fisherman. "We found it in the nets last night. It must be yours. Would you like it back?"

"Oh, yes, please!" said Anna.

"Thanks a lot!" shouted Matthew. "Come on, Anna! We've got just enough time to make another sandcastle before the tide comes in."

"But we'll bring the spade back this time," smiled Anna.

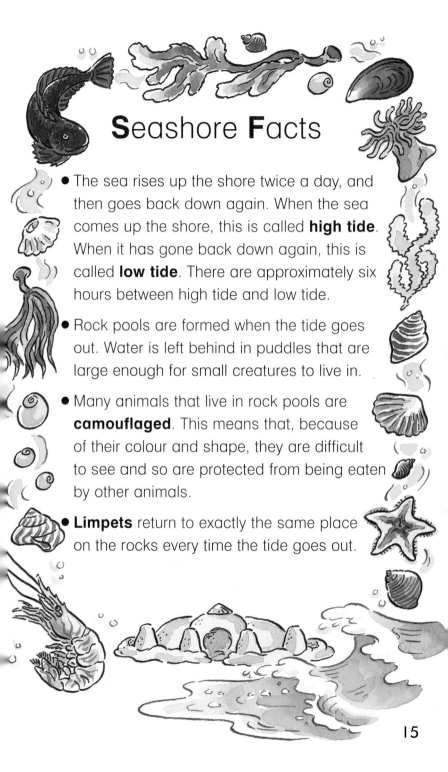

Seashore Facts

- The sea rises up the shore twice a day, and then goes back down again. When the sea comes up the shore, this is called **high tide**. When it has gone back down again, this is called **low tide**. There are approximately six hours between high tide and low tide.

- Rock pools are formed when the tide goes out. Water is left behind in puddles that are large enough for small creatures to live in.

- Many animals that live in rock pools are **camouflaged**. This means that, because of their colour and shape, they are difficult to see and so are protected from being eaten by other animals.

- **Limpets** return to exactly the same place on the rocks every time the tide goes out.

- Some beaches are pebbly and some are sandy. **Sand** is made of rocks and seashells that have been broken up by the sea into very small pieces. Black sand has either coal or volcanic rock in it. Sometimes, waves crash directly against cliffs, wearing them away to make caves and arches where the rock is soft.

- **Seaweed** has no roots, unlike a garden plant, but it can grip rocks so that it is not swept away by the sea. Some seaweed can survive out of water for a long time.

- The common prawn's favourite food is **sea lettuce**!

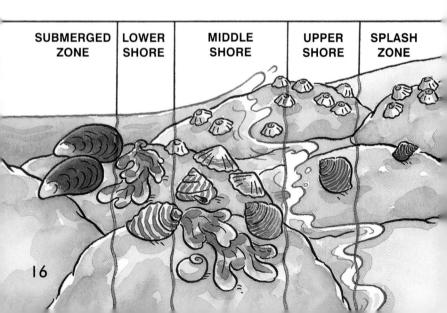

SUBMERGED ZONE	LOWER SHORE	MIDDLE SHORE	UPPER SHORE	SPLASH ZONE

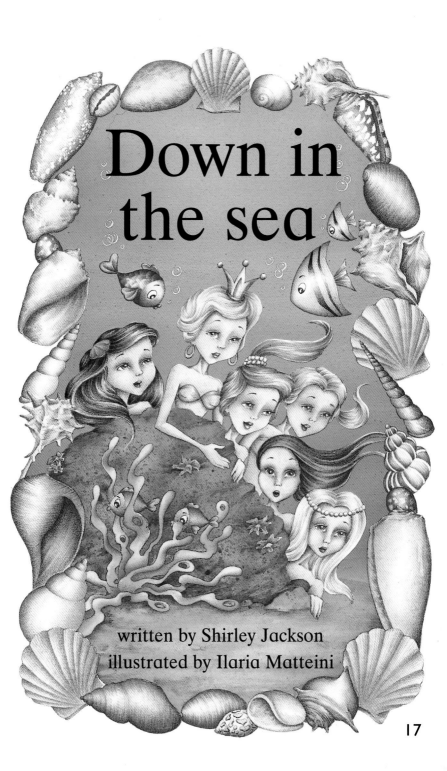

Down in the sea

written by Shirley Jackson
illustrated by Ilaria Matteini

Down in the sea,
where the seashells lie,

Six seahorses came
swimming by.

Down in the sea,
where the waters flow,

Six little mermaids
saw them go.

"I'll have the green one."
"I'll have the pink."
"I'll have the blue one.
What do you think?"

"I'll have the red one."
"The silver one's fine."
But the Sea Princess said,
"The gold one's mine."

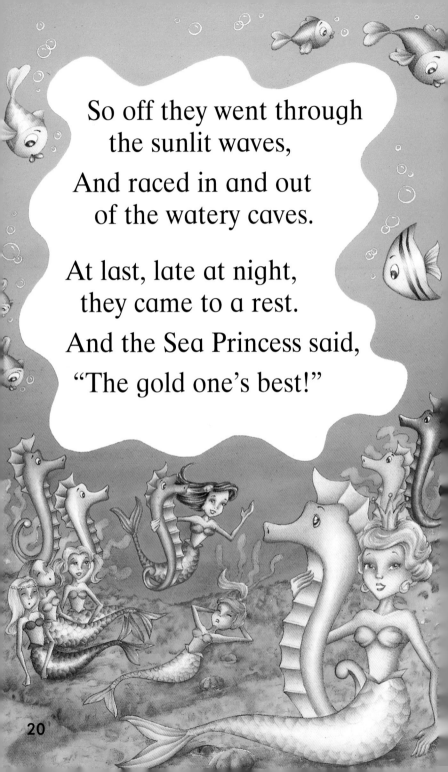

So off they went through
the sunlit waves,

And raced in and out
of the watery caves.

At last, late at night,
they came to a rest.

And the Sea Princess said,
"The gold one's best!"

Stop it
at once!

written by Lorraine Horsley
illustrated by Peter Stevenson

The photographer came to
school last Thursday.

We all folded our arms and smiled at the camera.

"Say 'Cheese'," said
the photographer.

Lucy Sanderson put up her hand.
"Please, Miss, Dennis Hill is
pulling my hair."

"Stop it at once, Dennis,"
said Mrs Taylor.

We all folded our arms and smiled at the camera.

"Say 'Cheese'," said the photographer.

Parul Patel put up her hand.
"Please, Miss, Dennis Hill is
pulling a funny face."

"Stop it at once, Dennis,"
said Mrs Taylor. "Please be
good or you'll have to sit
next to me."

We all folded our arms and smiled at the camera.

"Say 'Cheese'," said
the photographer.

Robert Johnson put up his hand. "Please, Miss, Dennis Hill is saying naughty things."

"Right, that's it!" said Mrs Taylor. "Dennis, come and sit by me."

We all folded our arms and
smiled at the camera for the
last time.

"Say 'Cheese'," said
the photographer.

Our class photo came today.
Mrs Taylor says it's the
best ever.

Dennis Hill's mum thinks it's
great too.

"You look like the best boy in
the class," she said.